GAY/CH

We hope you enjoy this book.
Please return or renew it by the due date.
You can renew it at **www.norfolk.gov.uk/libraries**
or by using our free library app. Otherwise you can
phone **0344 800 8020** - please have your library
card and pin ready.
You can sign up for email r~   too.

D0715733

Also in this series:

Cally & Jimmy: Twintastic

CALLY &JIMMY

TWINS IN TROUBLE

ZOE ANTONIADES

ILLUSTRATED BY KATIE KEAR

ANDERSEN PRESS

For Andrew

First published in 2020 by
Andersen Press Limited
20 Vauxhall Bridge Road
London SW1V 2SA
www.andersenpress.co.uk

2 4 6 8 10 9 7 5 3 1

All rights reserved. No part of this publication may be reproduced,
stored in a retrieval system or transmitted in any form, or by any means,
electronic, mechanical, photocopying, recording or otherwise,
without the written permission of the publisher.

The rights of Zoe Antoniades and Katie Kear to be identified as
the author and illustrator of this work have been asserted by them
in accordance with the Copyright, Designs and Patents Act, 1988.

Text copyright © Zoe Antoniades, 2020
Illustrations copyright © Katie Kear, 2020

British Library Cataloguing in Publication Data available.

ISBN 978 1 83913 008 3

This book is printed on FSC accredited
paper from responsible sources

Printed and bound in Great Britain by Clays Ltd, Elcograf S.p.A.

DOUBLE TROUBLE

DOUBLE DARE

DOUBLE ACT

DOUBLE DIGITS

DOUBLE TROUBLE

I have a twin brother. Everyone calls him Jimmy, which is sort of the English version of Dimitri, his actual Greek name. Our mum's Greek, you see, because our grandparents are from Cyprus. Dad's not Greek. He's from Clapham.

I'm Cally, short for Calista, which means, and I don't want to sound big-headed or anything, but it means 'most beautiful'. I'm not sure about Dimitri, but if Dimitri means most-annoying-brother-in-the-whole-wide-world, then that's him.

Because we're twins, I hardly ever get a break from him. I mean, we're even in the same class at school, cos it's one of those one-form-entry ones. Luckily, we don't have to sit next to each other. Jimmy has his own special table at the front, right next to the teacher's desk. I'm on the 'top table' at the back. It's not actually called that, but we know it is because we get the maths extension sheets and are all on the Independent Readers' books when everyone else is on Orange, Purple or Blue labels. Except for Jimmy. He goes out with our teaching assistant, Miss Loretta, to get his books from The Centre.

Even though we sit at total opposite ends of the classroom, I'm never allowed to forget he's there. Our teacher, Mrs Wright, calls his name out all the time to keep him on track. And if I'm not having to hear his name every five minutes, he's dropping his pencil on the floor, like, literally a hundred times an hour.

4

I mean, how hard is it to hold onto your pencil and just get on with your work? Very, if you're Jimmy George, is the answer to that.

He gets all the attention at home too. Not that either of us get that much attention from Mum anymore. She's always so busy working. She has two jobs now. It's not easy being a single parent, she says. But we don't only have one parent really, we still have Dad, it's just he doesn't live with us since they split up. But Yiayia does. She's our granny from Cyprus. She looks after us a lot, picks us up from school and all that. She says she loves us both very much and she loves us equally, but that's what you have to say to twins, isn't it? I know Jimmy's her favourite.

And Mum's too. Because whatever nonsense he gets up to, he always gets away with it, or somehow manages to get me in trouble as well. Double trouble, that's what people always say twins are. But it's not fair.

Mum's favourite thing to say to us is, 'You're both as bad as each other.' She said that last Sunday when everything went wrong . . .

There's this fix-it man who comes over to do jobs around the house. Mum likes him. I don't. He's called Grant and he thinks he's really cool and funny, but he absolutely 100 per cent isn't. Me and Jimmy don't agree about many things, but we definitely agree about that.

Sunday is the one day when we all get to be at home together, but Grant had come round to do some painting. We had to go through the embarrassment of watching Mum giggling and flicking her hair when she opened the door to him.

He winked at her and said, 'Hallo, Treacle.'

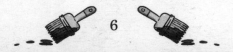

Mum laughed, even though he hadn't said anything funny. Why was she being like that?

Yiayia wouldn't have liked it, I'm sure. Luckily she'd been spared this cringe moment. She was asleep over her knitting in the front room. She's making a blanket for someone's brother-in-law's, auntie's cousin in Nicosia. Yiayia makes a lot of blankets.

'Thought I'd drop round and give the outside that coat of paint you've been wanting doing,' said Grant, like he was some great superhero.

'Ooh, bless you,' said Mum.

'Probably need to do something about in here too,' he said. Grant was looking the hallway up and down, frowning and shaking his head.

'Yes. I suppose the wallpaper does look a bit old-fashioned,' agreed Mum.

Actually, it didn't. Dad had decorated the hall not that long ago, just before he had to move out. There was nothing wrong with it.

'Who put that up for you, anyway? Must have been a right cowboy.'

Cowboy! That's my dad he was talking about.

Grant finally noticed me and Jimmy watching from the stairs. 'Hallo, kiddiewinks,' he said.

Kiddiewinks???

'Say hello to Grant,' chirped Mum.

'Hello, Grant,' we mumbled. Then we turned our backs and plodded up the stairs to our rooms. Jimmy went on his Xbox and I buried myself into my *Unicorn Diaries* while Grant went outside to paint the side wall of the house – like he was the greatest fix-it man the world had ever known. He was there all morning on his stupid ladder. And at one point he was at my window whenever I looked up from my book. So annoying.

After lunch, Mum hollered up the stairs, 'I'm just off out, kids. You'll be all right with your Yiayia now, won't you?'

I came out of my room and looked over the bannisters. Grant was standing there with Mum, he had his leather jacket on and his van keys in his hand.

'Where are you going?' I asked.

'Grant's taking me to DIY Express to pick out some new wallpaper for the hall.'

I didn't say anything. I just went back to my room.

What a boring, rubbish day it was turning out to be. I suddenly really missed my dad so I tried giving him a call, but there was no reply. Such a rubbish day.

I heard Jimmy get up from his gaming chair and cross the landing to the toilet. I was so bored, maybe it was time for a bit of fun. I decided to make Jimmy jump when he came out. Now I know that might make *me* sound

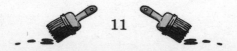

like the troublemaker, but it wasn't like that. He always does it to me too. It's just a game we play sometimes. We hide round corners, behind doors or under the furniture, then we spring out and yell, 'Raargh!' Once the shock wears off, we crack up – it's pretty funny.

Our toilet's one of those really tiny cupboard-like ones, separate from our bathroom. It's next to the stairs. So, I tiptoed over and lay in wait.

I waited and waited outside the toilet for him to finish but he was taking *ages*. This was going to be one of his long visits, if you know what I mean. He can sit there for ever sometimes, singing silly songs to himself.

So, there I was, silently waiting behind the wall, and there was Jimmy, on the other side, sitting on the toilet and yes, singing some stupid song Dad had taught him, on and on. When was he ever going to finish? I was getting a dead leg and pins and needles too. I was

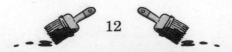

begging him to hurry up and shush up. Only in my head, of course. I didn't want him to know I was hiding out there, obviously. But it was as if he had some sort of sixth sense or something because, just at that moment, he stopped singing.

At last! He must have finished. I waited for the toilet to flush and poised myself, eyeballing the door, ready to pounce as soon as the handle turned. But the toilet didn't flush. And the door handle stayed still. What was he doing in there? It was beyond ages now, even for him. Ever so slowly, and ever so quietly, I edged my way round to face the door. One foot had gone totally numb so I balanced on my other foot and peered through the keyhole. The door still has one of those locks from the old days, but now we use a sliding latch thing from the inside instead and the original key is long gone. The actual keyhole is empty though and you can just about see through it if you want to.

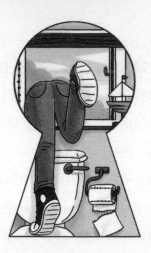

So, I peeped in, hoping that I wouldn't see Jimmy's . . . you know what.

But you'll never believe what I actually saw. Jimmy wasn't in there sitting on the toilet at all. He was climbing out of the tiny square window at the back. So, what I saw was just the soles of his trainers disappearing outside. He must have realised I was waiting to make him jump and had tried to outsmart me. Well, much as I hate to admit it, he pretty much had.

I guessed he was scrambling down the drainpipe. He's a bit of a monkey when it comes to that sort of thing. Always scaling trees and diving off things.

I was two things at once then. Firstly, I was scared he might hurt himself. But mostly, I was annoyed that he'd got the better of me. Well, two could play at that game.

I bolted down the stairs and out through the back door. And there he was with his back to me, shinning down the last leg of the drainpipe. When he landed and turned round and saw me standing right in front of him, he jumped out of his skin.

'Raargh!' I went.

'Aaaaaaagh!' went Jimmy.

We froze for a second, then fell about laughing.

'Tricked ya, though, didn't I?' he grinned, super pleased with himself.

'Tricked ya back.'

We turned to gaze up at the tiny toilet window which Jimmy had escaped from. And that's when our smiles were wiped right off our faces.

'Jimmmmmmyyyyy!' I gasped, in horror. 'Look what you did!'

Jimmy's jaw dropped.

All the way down Grant's freshly painted white wall, from the window to the ground, were Jimmy-shaped handprints and Jimmy-shaped footprints. And all over Jimmy was evidence of Grant's fresh paint.

'Mum's going to kill you,' I said.

Jimmy gulped, but then a moment later, he started marching towards the shed in the back garden.

'What're you doing?' I called after him.

'We'll have to paint it again, won't we?'

'What?!'

'Grant keeps all the leftover paint in the shed. Come on.'

I chased after him. Well, I didn't have much choice. I had a bad feeling in my belly about it, but I couldn't think of a better plan and Jimmy was already unbolting the shed door.

17

We aren't really allowed in the shed. It's full of rusty old tools and dented pots of paint, and the air has a toxic smell from that brown stuff for coating the fence with. It's jam-packed with our old bikes and a huge lawn mower and years' worth of junk. We could hardly move in there, but worst of all, there were cobwebs everywhere, all over the ceiling, in every corner and covering the dusty window. Which meant only one thing. Spiders.

'Let's hurry up, grab what we need and get out of here, Jimmy.'

Jimmy handed me a large tin of Grant's white paint and one of those roller things with a tray and I put them down on the grass. Getting the ladder out was not so easy. It was trapped behind all the other stuff. Jimmy made a right racket clambering over the bikes and the mower to reach it.

'Be careful, Jimmy. You're gonna wake up Yiayia.'

'You could try helping me instead of beefing about it then, couldn't you?'

He's so annoying! He was lucky I was there at all. It was him who'd got us into this mess. As always!

He pulled out the ladder and swung it round overhead.

'Jimmy, watch out!'

It only just missed the shed window.

Unfortunately, it didn't miss me.

'Ouch!'

'Sorry, Sis.'

'Whatever. Let's just get out of here and get this over with,' I grumbled.

Armed with the paint, roller and tray, and with the ladder between us, we marched back over to the house. We leaned the ladder against the wall and gazed up at the top. It seemed ever so high. But the wall was a right mess and it needed sorting before Mum and Grant got back.

Jimmy tried to get the lid off the paint. 'It's stuck,' he wheezed.

'Get something to yank it open with then,'
I said.

'Like what?'

'I dunno. Find something sharp.'

Jimmy dashed back to the shed – I stayed
where I was – I wasn't in any hurry to revisit
the spider den. He soon returned with a long
metal pole with a curved forked spike on the end.

'That's a bit extreme, isn't it?'

'Can't see you coming up with any better
ideas,' huffed Jimmy and he started trying to
wrench open the paint-pot lid. It came away all
right. *Bam!* There was an explosion of paint,
which splattered all over my leggings and top.
My favourite unicorn-rainbow top!

But Jimmy ignored me and started tipping the paint into the tray like Grant does. Then he rolled the roller thingy in it, sloshing it about and making a right mess of that too.

'This is a really bad idea, Jimmy. I think we should just stop.'

'It's cool, Sis. It's cool. I've got this. You just hold the ladder steady.'

Again, I had no choice. Jimmy was already clambering up the ladder, roller in one hand, and holding on with the other. I was terrified. How could he do that one-handed? The ladder wobbled and creaked as Jimmy continued up to the top. He started covering over the messed-up paintwork with the roller. Actually, the first few goes weren't that bad. But then there was a giant scuff that was a bit further away.

'Why don't you come down and we'll move the ladder over a bit?' I suggested.

'Nah. It's OK. I reckon if I just . . . stretch . . . I can just . . . reach . . .'

And that's when Jimmy lost his footing. He dropped the paint roller (which landed on my head) and grabbed the ladder with both hands. But he still went sliding down . . . down . . . down, landing with an almighty crash – one foot skidding through the tray, and the other finishing smack bang in the middle of the pot of paint.

It was the worst timing ever because Mum and Grant literally got back at that moment. They must have heard the noise because they came running, with Yiayia as well, and gawped at the total devastation. And they clearly didn't see the funny side. Yiayia clipped Jimmy round the ear and said, 'What you thinking? You could to be break your neck.'

Grant just stood there looking us and the wall up and down, frowning and shaking his head.

Mum started yelling at us, 'Look what you've done to my newly-painted wall! And your clothes! And your shoes!'

And Jimmy got straight in with his excuses, pointing at me and saying, 'It was Cally. She . . . she . . . she started it. She was the one who wouldn't even leave me alone to go to the toilet . . .'

'What?!' I was furious. 'Don't blame me. Who was it that climbed out the window? Who was it that mucked up the wall? Who was it that wanted to get the paint?'

'You're both as bad as each other,' snapped Mum.

I told you she always says that. It's so unfair. We clearly aren't.

'And don't think you're not going to have to face the consequences,' added Mum. 'Grant's

going to have to repaint the wall. That's coming out of your allowance. Money doesn't grow on trees you know.'

Losing our pocket money was bad enough. But having Grant ganging up on us with Mum was even worse. I knew he'd have something 'clever' to say about what we'd done as well, once he'd finished with all that frowning and shaking his head business.

'And that's not all. You'll be doing double chores for a month,' Mum continued.

'NOOOOOO!'

'But . . . but . . .' I said.

'There's no buts about it. Now get yourselves upstairs and cleaned up. Yiayia is going to have to scrub you both. That paint won't come off easily you know.'

As we sloped off inside, I heard Mum saying, 'I despair, Grant, I really do. As if I haven't got enough on my plate!'

And yet again he made the most out of the situation and tried to be a superhero. 'You're doing a great job, Stella. Now, let's get another coat of paint on that wall, shall we?' I bet he was putting his arm round her too. Talk about puke.

I stormed into my bedroom and sat there fuming. My hair was covered in paint. I couldn't read. I couldn't listen to music. And not even my favourite cuddly unicorn that Dad got me for Christmas a few years ago helped. Nothing would make me feel better about this. It was all wrong. And it was all Jimmy's fault.

I could hear him in the bathroom as Yiayia tried to get the paint off. Complaining and blubbering the whole time. 'Oh, Yiayia, don't scrub so hard. Please, Yiayia, you're hurting. Do you have to use that nasty cleaning stuff? It stinks. Noooo, you've got soap in my eyes!'

Good, I thought to myself. *Such a baby.*

When he'd finished his bath, and all his dramatics, he had the cheek to turn up at my room. He poked his head round the door and said, 'It's your turn in the bathroom now. Yiayia's waiting.'

I turned away from him. 'Look, I'm sorry, Sis.'

'Sorry, Sis. Sorry, Sis,' I said, doing an impression of his pathetic voice. 'Sometimes, Jimmy, sorry isn't good enough. Sometimes, it would be nice if you didn't have to always wreck things in the first place.'

We could hear Grant up the ladder outside the toilet window again, whistling some out-of-tune rubbish song.

'Hey, why don't we creep up to the window and make him jump?' grinned Jimmy.

'Yeah, why don't we just get ourselves in even bigger trouble?' I said, shoving him out of the way and heading off to the bathroom.

Yiayia was coming out to find me and as she crossed the landing, Grant started trying to whistle a Greek tune through the toilet window. Her shoulder 'accidentally' caught the door as she went by and it slammed in his face. Not whistling any more after that, was he?

Yiayia looked at me and I looked at Yiayia and we both knew we were trying not to laugh.

She scooped her arm round my shoulder and steered me into the bathroom.

'Come on, Calista mou. Let's be wash your hair.'

Yiayia was a bit rough with trying to get all the paint out, and the stuff she used did smell horrible, but then she used her special olive and orange-blossom shampoo and conditioner on me and I felt a lot better after that.

As I was drying off, the phone rang. Dad! It had to be.

I ran downstairs in my bathrobe yelling, 'I'll get it!' just beating Jimmy to it. I stuck my tongue out at Jimmy as I lifted the receiver.

'Yeah . . . Hi, Dad . . . no, not really . . . I'd just tried to phone you before cos I was a bit bored . . . No, everything's OK really . . . Yeah, really . . . It's just been what you'd call "one of those days" . . . No, Jimmy just got us in trouble again, as usual . . .'

'It was an accident!' Jimmy was hopping

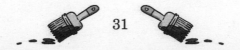

31

from one foot to the next trying to grab the phone out of my hands.

'... All right, I'll put him on,' I said, passing Jimmy the phone. 'Dad wants to talk to you.'

'Dad, it wasn't ... Yeah ... I suppose ... OK ... I'll try to be more good ... Yeah ... I love you as well, Dad. Bye.'

Grant walked through the door just as the phone call ended. At the same time, Yiayia came bustling into the downstairs hall, with a towel in one hand and the bottle of her disgusting cleaning stuff in the other. She took one look at Grant's paint-splattered boots and overalls and began waving him back out of the door.

'You no come inside like that. What you doing? You making big mess. Is enough mess already.' She shoved the towel and bottle of cleaner in his hands and said, 'Is tap outside. You go wash there, dirty man.' It didn't look like she'd be sharing her olive and orange-blossom shampoo and conditioner with him any time soon.

Me and Jimmy ran into the living room and burst out laughing.

'Ha ha! Grant got told off by Yiayia.'

'Did you see his face!'

And suddenly, I wasn't cross with Jimmy any more. I guess with people like Grant around, me and Jimmy have to stick together. That's what twins do.

DOUBLE DARE

Whenever it's home time, we all run out into the playground to find our mums or dads or whoever it is that's collecting us. For me and Jimmy it's always Yiayia, because Mum works full-time and Dad lives too far away now. Jimmy usually comes bolting out with his hands in the air, yelling, 'Freeeedom!' then he does a celebratory lap around the AstroTurf or something.

But the other day, he came out all hot and upset. There were streaks running through the smudges on his cheeks from where he'd been crying too. Yiayia held her arms open and he buried his head in her black, knitted shawl.

'Mana mou, Jimmy. What happen?' said Yiayia, stroking his scruffy hair.

'I hate Mrs Gutteridge!'

To be fair to Jimmy, no one likes Mrs Gutteridge very much.

Yiayia unburied my brother, put her hands on his shoulders and looked him in the eye.

'Hate is very strong word, Jimmy mou. You must not to talk about the teachers like that.'

'She's not even a teacher, she's a dinner lady. And she made me sit on the bench and miss most of playtime for NOTHING! And it was our class's turn on the football pitch!'

'Maybe she think you do something, Jimmy,' said Yiayia, rummaging around in her pocket and pulling out a fluffy tissue.

'But I didn't. She's the rubbishest dinner lady ever.' Jimmy clenched his fists and kicked the ground.

Yiayia looked to me for an explanation. This is one of the downsides of being a twin. Always being together. You end up having to live through all the chaos your hyper brother makes. Except I'm not meant to call him hyper. It's ADHD he's got. Sometimes I think that's his excuse for being annoying. Anyway, that's why he gets all the attention all the time.

That's why he gets let off for things that the rest of us would totally get told off for. Except this time Mrs Gutteridge did tell him off and that's why Jimmy was in such a rage. And there was Yiayia, still looking at me for answers.

'Well . . . the thing is, Yiayia . . . when Mrs Gutteridge rang the bell for the kids having packed lunches to line up, Jimmy ran over really fast and ended up crashing into everyone . . .'

'How do *you* know? You weren't even there! You were inside doing posters for the bake sale, like the teacher's pet that you are,' snapped Jimmy.

I knew he was just jealous because he never gets chosen to do stuff like that. Special opportunities like lunch-time passes and monitor duties don't come Jimmy's way very often. The bake sale was the next day and I'd had a great time helping with the posters for it, only to come back at the end of lunch time to have it all ruined by everyone saying,

'Did you hear what your brother's done?' and, 'Jimmy's in big trouble,' and, 'Jimmy's had one of his epic rages again.'

'Just because I wasn't there, doesn't mean I don't still know what you did,' I told him. 'It's not like half the entire school wasn't talking about it. Always showing me up. Why do you keep pushing into everyone anyway?'

'It wasn't everyone!' yelled Jimmy. 'It was only Nina who fell down and it was an accident.'

'Yeah, right, only an accident for the fifth time this week,' I reminded him. 'You know you can't ever line up properly, that's why we have a lining-up order and you're meant to be at the front.'

Jimmy's face was like thunder, so I didn't go on to tell Yiayia that it was interesting how he only ever seemed to 'accidentally' barge into the nice, little kids like Nina Wilinska and never the big kids like Mitch Moran.

Yiayia made the sign of the cross (a sort of prayer thing old lady Greek people do all the time), looked to the heavens and gave up. She hooked her arm into Jimmy's and led us home.

When we got back to the house, Jimmy stormed up to his room and slammed the door. I know that often brothers or sisters like it when the other one's in trouble and not them, but this time I was actually a bit on Jimmy's side and I felt bad for snaking him out to Yiayia. Mrs Gutteridge definitely tells people off too much. She has these giant pockets in her skirt which she says are perfect for confiscating things – little toys, bits of Lego, trading cards, sweets and all that. And one time, when I wasn't feeling very well, and I even had a note from my mum to say that I could stay inside and just read, Mrs Gutteridge still made me go out in the cold. And if it's ever wet play and everyone does have to stay inside, she never lets us get the games out and do what we want. Instead she makes us all sit together on the carpet for a sing-song. Totally cringe. And she's so old, the songs are never ones we've heard of or they're, like, nursery rhymes. Once she sang us this stupid lullaby to supposedly calm us down. Except her voice was all wobbly and the words were so babyish. *Tragicccc*. And we were, like, 'We're in Year Five, you know.'

Anyway, I gave Jimmy a bit of time to cool off, then went upstairs and knocked gently on his door.

'Go away.'

Still in a grump then.

I tried again, 'It's only me, Jimmy. Let me in. Come on. You were a bit annoying, but you didn't deserve to miss football.'

I could hear him shuffling about and soon

after, the door opened and he was standing in front of me with his snotty face.

'Don't cry anymore, Jimmy. Let's do something to cheer you up. I know, let's ask Yiayia if we can make some cakes now for the bake sale tomorrow.'

Jimmy wiped his nose on his sleeve and smiled. And before I knew it, he was tearing down the stairs calling, 'Yiayia . . .!'

I followed him into the sitting room to find him pulling Yiayia up from her armchair and startling her out of her snooze.

'Gently, Jimmy mou, gently please.' My poor granny always has to put up with so much when it comes to Jimmy.

'We need to make some cakes, Yiayia. For the bake sale. It's tomorrow,' insisted Jimmy, hopping about like a ballistic bunny.

'Is tomorrow? Why you no say before?' said Yiayia, rubbing her forehead.

Jimmy did this puppy-eyed thing that always works with Yiayia and she caved in immediately. 'All right, all right. So, what we do? We make Greek cakes, yes? Baklava or bourekki?'

'It's all right, Yiayia,' I said. 'I know how to make brownies by myself. Mum lets me now. You just need to help us with the oven part. I'll make the cakes with Jimmy. You have your sleep.'

'I no sleeping. I just rest my eyes,' said Yiayia. She always says that. She knows we think it's funny. So she winked at us, pulled her favourite homemade blanket over her knees, and settled herself back down.

Jimmy raced into the kitchen and opened up all the cupboards looking for ingredients and equipment. He'd have emptied the whole lot out everywhere if it wasn't for me.

'Slow down, Jimmy,' I said. 'We only need one bowl . . . and put those raisins back . . . and all that other stuff . . . we're only making brownies, not half a bakery shop.'

'You never let me do anything, Miss Bossy Pants,' huffed Jimmy. 'Anyway. I thought you were supposed to be cheering me up.'

'Look. I'll let you do all the weighing and the stirring and stuff, you just have to let me be in charge, cos I *am* the one who actually knows how to do these things properly. Right . . . now then . . . we need 225 grams of plain flour . . .'

Sticking his tongue out of the side of his mouth (he does that when he is in deep concentration – which isn't that often with Jimmy), he ever so carefully measured the ingredients one by one. We were doing Dad's 'fool-proof recipe' which means you can pretty much chuck everything together and mix it all up in one go, and so even Jimmy was able to manage that without too much of a disaster. Pretty soon we had a fantastically gooey, chocolatey brownie batter going on.

'Wow! Check it out,' said Jimmy, looking very pleased with himself.

I was glad he was feeling better about everything now.

'She's so annoying though, Mrs Gutteridge, isn't she?' said Jimmy as he stirred everything around.

Not completely over it then.

'And a bit weird too,' he continued. 'Like how she always takes the cups away before anyone's even finished.'

'And she'll never let you go out to play until you've eaten every single scrap of food,' I said, joining in, 'even if you don't like it. The way she inspects your lunch, sniffing it and eyeballing it, then telling you how lovely it is.'

'Yeah, and if you still don't want it, she even goes and takes a bit off your plate and eats it herself.'

'Now that's totally weird,' I had to agree.

And then, suddenly, 'That's it!' he said.

'What's it?' I asked, raising an eyebrow. Jimmy had come up with one of his risky ideas, I could tell.

'How about we put something nasty in the brownies, and instead of taking them to the bake sale, we sneak one into our packed lunch and get old Gutter-bags to eat it off our plate?'

'Jimmy, you're evil,' I said.

'Come on, Sis. It'll be funny.'

'Sort of . . .'

'And we are still trying to cheer me up, aren't we?'

Once again, I was finding myself somehow getting completely caught up in the middle of another Jimmy situation. 'OK . . .' I agreed. 'What shall we put in then?'

'How about a spider? Bet there's one down the back of the fridge or something . . .' said Jimmy, already getting down on his hands and knees to search for one.

'No way!' I shrieked, pulling him back. I'm terrified of spiders.

'All right then. Maybe something from the cleaning cupboard, or the shed, or the bins!'

'That might be taking it just a bit too far, Jimmy. We might want to trick her, but we don't want to actually kill her.'

And then we both seemed to notice it at once. There on the shelf by the window. A tall brown, sticky bottle with a mustard-yellow label.

'Yiayia's prune juice!'

For ages we weren't exactly sure what Yiayia's prune juice was for. She only ever says it's 'to make her regular'. So one day we made Mum tell us. She explained that Yiayia needs it to make her do a number two. Gross! And I think that must be right because one time she forgot she'd taken some and had double and ended up on the toilet all afternoon. Yiayia calls it her 'special medicine'. It's not meant to be dangerous like tablets or anything, but it looks yuk. Like black sludge.

'It would be totally camouflaged in the brownie mix, wouldn't it?' said Jimmy, clapping his hands.

'Let's do it,' I said. I know, I know, I shouldn't have done it, but Jimmy just has this way of making things seem like a good idea at the time.

Jimmy held out the bowl ceremoniously, 'Pour it in then.'

See. He even managed to make *me* be the one to put the prune juice in.

I hesitated for a moment, but then, *slosh!* In it went. Jimmy stirred the mixture vigorously, his tongue poking out the side of his mouth in serious concentration once more.

'Ta da! All done,' he said with pride. It had blended together perfectly. No one would ever know. We stared at the bowl in wonder. And then Jimmy's nose began to twitch.

'Aaaaaah chooo!'

'Brilliant!' cheered Jimmy. 'Now it's even got my snot-spray molecules in it.'

'Jimmy, you're gross!' But deep down I had to admit it was actually the ultimate finishing touch.

We dolloped the mixture into a tray and called for Yiayia to help us put it in the oven. She shuffled into the kitchen admiring our work. 'Bravo, children, is beautiful, bravo,' she said. And me and Jimmy burst out laughing.

In the oven the tray went. The two of us sat silently on little stools, watching the brownies through the glass door as they baked under the glow of the oven lamp.

After they were done and they'd cooled down on the wire rack, we dusted them with icing sugar. They looked amazing. Good enough to eat. Except there'd only be one person eating them tomorrow, and that was Mrs Gutteridge.

We arranged them in a fancy cardboard box, lined with a doily, and perched them proudly on the worktop. Tomorrow we'd take them to school, pretending they were for the bake sale, but really the plan was to put one in our packed lunch and then chuck the rest away. Jimmy patted the lid of the box and grinned. 'It's payback time!'

That night, I woke up from a bad dream. I couldn't exactly remember what it was about, but I knew it was bad because it left me with a tight feeling in my belly. The red light-up numbers on my digital clock said 3:00am.

The middle of the night. I lay in bed trying to get back to sleep but I just couldn't. I switched on my toadstool lamp and tried reading a bit of my book, but I got through two or three pages without even knowing what I'd read. I tried again over and over, but my mind just wouldn't fix on the story. I switched off the light and lay back on my pillow staring at the ceiling. I tried counting the glow-in-the-dark stars I've got stuck on there. I lost count. I was still wide awake. I tossed and turned in my bed until my unicorn duvet was a twisted mess.

A door creaked. Was Mum coming? I lay dead still and shut my eyes – pretending. I listened carefully. Yiayia was softly snoring in her bed downstairs. Mum was mumbling in her sleep in her room at the end of the landing. It wasn't them then. The door creaked again. Then footsteps. And Jimmy poked his head round my door and rubbed his eyes.

'You can't sleep either then?' I said.

'I can't stop thinking about them cakes.'
He sat down cross-legged at the end of my bed
and fiddled with his toes.

'We've got guilty consciences, haven't we?'
I explained. 'That's why we can't sleep.'

'We might poison her. She might even die!'
Jimmy was always so dramatic.

'We only put Yiayia's prune juice in there . . .'

'. . . and my snot-spray.'

'I suppose even Mrs Gutteridge doesn't deserve that, does she?' I reasoned. 'And you did push into the line again. She was allowed to tell you off really, wasn't she? She was just protecting the other kids. If you think about it, she can be quite kind sometimes.'

'Yeah, like when she puts magic cream on the little kids' knees if they fall over on the playground . . .'

'. . . And if someone's sitting on their own on the bench, she goes over and chats to them . . .'

'. . . And she always watches your singing and dancing acts at playtime when you ask her to . . .'

'. . . And even that lullaby, it might be a bit babyish, but it's kind of sweet of her to want to sing to us really.'

We both let out a deep sigh at the same time. If we weren't feeling so ashamed and so exhausted, we might have laughed at that.

'So, we're not going to poison her, then?' said Jimmy.

'No, Jimmy, I don't think we'll be giving her any of those brownies. We'll just accidentally-on-purpose leave them behind in the morning.'

'Good idea, Cals,' said Jimmy.

'Well, one of us has to have them,' I said, pushing him off my bed.

'Night, night,' he said, shuffling back to his room.

I snuggled down into my pillow and the next thing I knew, it was morning.

★

Mum had left everything we needed for school, ready for us, by the top of the stairs. Book bags, my violin, our PE kits and a note to say that our lunch boxes were in the fridge and not to forget the brownies that were on the worktop in the kitchen – with a 'P.S. They look beautiful by the way.' I quickly screwed up the note before Yiayia saw it and chucked it in the bin as I went to get our packed lunches.

It's always a bit of a mad dash to get out of the door, even with Mum being more organised than a sergeant major. Jimmy had got Yiayia in her usual spin – running around at the last minute trying to find a comb for his sticky-uppy hair – so it was easy for the brownies to go accidentally-on-purpose unnoticed as, loaded up with our bags, cases and boxes and an already worn-out granny, we hurried off to school.

At registration, anyone who had something for the bake sale had to take it to the office. Lots of children had brought cakes in, so it didn't matter too much that we didn't have any. I made up my mind to ask Yiayia to take us to buy cakes from the sale after school when she came to pick us up, that way we'd still be giving something towards the charity.

When it was lunch time, both me and Jimmy couldn't help being extra nice to Mrs Gutteridge. I even offered to help with the little ones who were super slow at eating their dinner.

'That's very kind of you, poppet,' she said. 'You sit with them until they've finished, then you can help tidy away their trays and take them back to the infant playground.'

'I can help too, if you like, Mrs Gutteridge,' Jimmy offered.

Mrs Gutteridge looked a bit shocked for a moment, but then she just patted Jimmy on the head and said, 'That's OK, pet, I think you might be better off having a good run around outside before the bell goes.'

For the rest of the day I just got on quietly with my work at the top table, apart from when it was time to go out for my violin lesson. Jimmy doesn't do violin anymore. Yiayia once said it sounded like he was strangling a cat. He gave up soon after that. I'm taking my Grade Two next summer, which my dad says is really impressive. When we go to visit him every other weekend, he always asks me to play my tunes for him.

At the end of the day, when we were all in the playground and Jimmy was busy making his lap of honour around the pitch hollering,

'Freeeedom!'

I was looking around for Yiayia. I couldn't see her anywhere. So, I yanked Jimmy off the AstroTurf and took us both up to the office, which is what you have to do if no one comes to collect you.

The secretary saw us coming and said, 'Are you looking for your grandma? Not to worry. She's already here. She popped in just now with your cakes. I've sent her round to the hall to put them with the others. I must say, they look terrific. Brownies. My favourite!'

Jimmy's jaw dropped. So did mine. We looked at each other and went, 'Aargh!' at exactly the same time. We made a dash for the hall. But it was too late. There they stood, in pride of place, on the top cake stand on the top table. And this was one top table I did *not* want to be on right now.

Yiayia greeted us with open arms. 'Hello, Cally mou. Hello, Jimmy mou. You forget you cakes. You see? I bring you cakes.'

We stood there, struck with horror. What were we going to do?

'Come on, Jimmy,' I said through gritted teeth, 'if ever there's a time for one of your fancy plans, this is it.'

And then a light bulb went on in Jimmy's head. I could see it in his eyes. He whispered in my ear, 'You go line up at the cake stall, I'll do the rest.'

I wasn't sure what his plan was, but I was desperate. I asked Yiayia for two pounds and went over to where everyone was queuing.

Please don't anyone buy the brownies, please don't anyone buy the brownies, please don't anyone buy the brownies . . .

As this went round and round in my head, I sensed something come charging up to me. It all happened so fast. Then the something crashed into me. And the force of that something sent me hurtling headfirst into the pile of cakes. A direct hit.

Jimmy yelled,

'BOOOOOOM!'

Of course, it had to have been Jimmy. Jimmy with his famous 'pushing into the line' trick.

I peeled myself up from the cake table, covered in crumbs and cream. Everything on the top table had been smashed to smithereens. And everyone was pointing at me and laughing. Well, not quite everyone . . .

'Jimmy George!' Mrs Gutteridge came marching over. 'Look at what you've done to your sister. Not to mention our beautiful display. It's a disgrace. How many times have we talked about lining up properly? What would make you do such a thing?'

If only she knew! He'd saved her, and everyone else, from the dodgy cakes. And in true Jimmy style too.

Jimmy just stood there opening and closing his mouth like a goldfish.

Yiayia came scurrying over, looking confused, shocked, ashamed and concerned all at the same time. She found me a fuzzy tissue from her handbag to wipe my face with and put her arm across Jimmy's shoulders. Then she apologised to Mrs Gutteridge, 'Is not his fault, you see? He has this D-A-H-D-H.'

Mrs Wright came up to smooth things over. She was trying to put on her serious-teacher-face, but the corners of her mouth kept turning up. 'Perhaps you should all go home and let it blow over,' she said.

Yiayia got out her purse and pressed a five-pound note into Mrs Wright's hand.

'Oh no, really, there's no need for that,' she said.

'Yes. Yes. Please. Take. Is for cakes. Is for charity,' insisted my kind, sweet, lovely Yiayia. And that completed our grand contribution to the charity bake sale.

Me and Jimmy will always remember that day. We still like making cakes together, but one thing is for certain, we'll never, ever add a secret ingredient, ever again.

DOUBLE ACT

After half term, Mrs Wright announced that it was our class's turn to do the special assembly. *Yesssss!* A ripple of excitement ran around the room. There'd be acting parts, new songs to learn and costumes to wear. Even for those who didn't like attention and being on stage there'd still be loads they could get involved with, Mrs Wright said, and we all knew it would mean no boring lessons for a few days.

'It's going to be *Jack and the Beanstalk*,' she told us.

And instantly everything fell flat.

Jimmy couldn't help himself and let out an enormous groan.

It was how we all felt, but Nina Wilinska was a bit more tactful and put up her hand and quietly said, 'Aren't we a bit big for fairy tales? We *are* in Year Five now.'

'There's more to it than that,' explained Mrs Wright. 'Trust me. They don't call me "Mrs Never-Wrong" for nothing you know.'

It's true. People do call her that. But I think she made it up herself in the first place.

 78

Mrs Wright enjoys experimenting with words and she thinks we all should too. Luckily I'm pretty good at creative writing. I'm even better at maths – I get that from Dad – but I'm top in English too. I don't want to sound big-headed but it's true. I even won a creative writing competition in Year Four. The prize was a really nice pen – but Jimmy broke it when he was cross one day. It took me a long time to forgive him for that.

Jimmy hates writing. He says it's boring. And if something is boring then he won't concentrate. Miss Loretta always has to bribe him with the computer to get him to write more than two sentences.

'We're going to re-write *Jack and the Beanstalk* with a twist. An alternative fairy tale if you like.'

'I don't like,' Jimmy blurted out.

Mrs Wright tried her best to ignore that. Anyone else would have had a table-point taken off them for being rude, but Jimmy is given chances. Too many, if you ask me, but no-one ever does. Jimmy can't help it, apparently. He's special, we're always being told. Aren't the rest of us special too?

It turned out that we were going to plan the story together and Mrs Wright was going to act as 'scribe', which meant she was going to do all the actual writing, so Jimmy would be OK after all. He can be quite entertaining when he has to come up with ideas.

Mrs Wright gathered us all together on the carpet (Jimmy sat on his own special cushion by her feet) and she set up the interactive whiteboard.

'So, this is how it works,' she began. 'We start telling the story as most of us know it, but then we begin to change things. It could be one of the characters, or the setting, or maybe the solution to the problem . . .' As she began to type the introduction into her computer, the story took shape on the screen.

Jack was a young lad who lived in a village with his mother. They were very poor.

So poor, in fact, that it came to be that Jack must sell the last thing of value that they owned. Their beloved cow, Daisy . . .

'Now "Daisy" is a very traditional name for a cow,' said Mrs Wright, pausing at the keyboard, 'so shall we start by changing that? Any alternative suggestions?'

'How about Calista?' suggested Jimmy.

Everyone started laughing. I was fuming.

'Now, Jimmy, that's not very nice,' said Mrs Wright. But I'm sure she was smiling too. 'I don't think we should give the cow your sister's name.'

'But it means "most beautiful",' he said. And then everyone started laughing even more.

'How about Michelle?' suggested my best friend Aisha Khan.

Everyone thought that was hilarious too. Mrs Wright smiled. 'That's the spirit, Aisha. It's meant to be funny. Michelle it is,' and she continued to tap at the keyboard.

Luckily everyone seemed to forget about calling her Calista. But I still glared across the room at Jimmy.

Their beloved cow, Michelle, was all they had left. So that morning, Jack, with a heavy heart, was sent off to market with strict instructions from his mother to get the best price he could for it.

Nina put up her hand.

'Yes, Nina?'

'Why were they poor, Miss? Maybe we could put something in our new version about that . . .'

'Maybe . . .' joined in Mitch Moran, 'maybe it's because of the giant. Maybe, it's because he has all the gold stashed away in his castle and wants it all for himself, because he's mean and miserable.'

'And the only way to get it back is to cheer him up,' I said, picking up the thread. 'But everyone in the village is too scared to try, because if ever someone fails, he just eats them.'

Mrs Wright was beaming from ear to ear, as she tapped it all into the computer. Her fingers were practically dancing on the keyboard.

However, on the way to market, Jack met a mysterious man who persuaded him to trade Michelle for some magic beans . . .

 84

The story carried on as normal for a bit after that, with Jack's mum going crazy because he'd come back with rubbish old beans instead of cash, and her throwing them out of the window into the yard.

'So, what happens next?' asked Mrs Wright. 'There's no need for a beanstalk that grows up into the clouds, as our giant lives in a castle near the village. So, what do the beans grow into instead?'

Jimmy burst out with, 'Weeeeeeds! Loads of tangly, stringy, weedy weeds. Then Jack's mum will totally go nuts.'

Everyone roared with laughter. We were laughing *with* Jimmy though, not at him.

'Well done, Jimmy. You're catching on brilliantly. This is what alternative tales do. Whilst the readers are expecting the beans to grow into a magnificent towering beanstalk, all they get is a pitiful pile of weeds.'

'And then . . . and then . . .' Jimmy was

getting really excited now. So excited that he was springing up off his cushion and Mrs Wright had to gently pat his shoulder to shrink him back down again. 'And then . . . Michelle the cow comes back because she's been missing Jack so much. She's escaped from the weird-magic-bean-man in the middle of the night and the next morning Jack and his mum wake up to find Michelle munching on all the weeds in the yard. *Munch, munch, munch.* And then . . . and then because the weeds are made from the magic beans, they give Michelle magic powers and so she . . . and so she . . . and so she . . . can DANCE!'

By this point Jimmy had bounced up from his cushion and was dancing about on the carpet. He was treading on Nina a bit and Mrs Wright had to keep shielding everyone from his windmill arms, but he was unstoppable. He was owning this story now. 'And the dancing cow is *so* the best dancer in all the land and it's extra amazing because she's a cow and all that, so Michelle goes to the castle and dances for the moody giant and the giant is all happified and he gives Jack a ton of gold and now they're rich

and they all live happily ever after – and we have to call the story *Jack and the Weedstalks* – The End!'

The whole class cheered and whooped and clapped. Mrs Wright clapped hardest of all. She gave Jimmy ten extra table-points and he got half an hour on the computers with Miss Loretta for it too. I felt pretty proud of him.

Normally it feels like he's making lessons harder for everyone, not coming up with good ideas. Except for the Calista the cow idea, of course.

Mrs Wright promised us that she'd work on the script that night so that we could get started as soon as possible.

The next morning, as we all lined up, we couldn't wait for the bell to go so we could find out what parts we'd got. Not that there'd be any surprises for me. I was bound to be a narrator. The Independent Readers always are. I don't mind that much, but it might be nice to be one of the characters for a change. The teachers say it's because I'm reliable. But Jimmy says it's because I'm a boring nerd.

Mrs Wright did have a different kind of surprise waiting for us though. There, in the middle of the carpet, was a giant cow. A proper professional-looking one like you get in the pantomimes. A costume that two whole people could get inside.

 89

Everyone was pointing and shrieking and gasping and running over to it.

'It's massive!'

'Is that for our play?'

'AWESOME!'

'No, it's for flying to outer space in, you doughnut, what do you think it's for?'

Mrs Wright shook her tambourine in the air, which is what she does to get us to be quiet and go back to our places. She had to shake it about a billion times to calm us down but at last we did.

'Year Five, meet Michelle. Michelle, meet Year Five,' she said.

'Who's gonna be in it?'

'Can I?'

'Can I?'

Jimmy was bursting out of his seat. He was doing that thing where he puts one hand under his other elbow so he can push his arm higher than anyone else's. And he was muttering, 'Me, me, me!' as he strained.

'Me, me, me!'

I knew he'd be desperate for that part cos he loves dancing, but I don't think I'd ever seen him want anything so badly before. 'Please, Miss,' he said. 'Please can I be Michelle? It was my idea to make it a dancing cow.'

Mrs Wright looked a bit awkward. I knew what she was thinking. It took two people to be a pantomime cow like that one, and it would be a nightmare to get Jimmy to work together properly with anyone else inside that costume.

'The thing is, Jimmy, it takes a lot of co-ordination and teamwork to get a pantomime cow to even walk in the right direction, let alone dance . . .' she tried to explain.

'Please, please, please, Miss. I'll practise with my partner every day. They can come to my house after school and everything . . .'

'Well . . . er . . . let's see . . .' Mrs Wright looked doubtfully around the classroom for a possible other half for my brother. 'Who'd like to volunteer to work with Jimmy, then?'

Everyone started looking at the floor, or up at the ceiling or fiddling with their pencil cases. Nina shrank down so far in her seat that she practically disappeared under the table. A minute ago, all those kids would have died for a chance to be Michelle. But now . . . It's not that they didn't like Jimmy. It's just, well, when it came to teamwork, well, Jimmy was Jimmy.

Jimmy turned round in his seat and gazed up at me at the top table. Even though he was all the way down there at the front of the classroom, I could see his eyes were welling up. Poor Jimmy. He might be annoying a lot of the time but he's still my brother.

Half-heartedly raising my hand, and more than half-choking on my words, I said, 'I suppose, I could do it.'

'Of course. Twins. Excellent. The perfect double act. Now why didn't I think of that in the first place?'

 94

Because I was always the narrator. Because this was a disaster waiting to happen. Because this was Jimmy George as a dancing pantomime cow! Oh well, at least I would be getting a character part for once. Sort of.

Miss Loretta took me and Jimmy out to have a practice. The cow costume was white and fluffy with brown patches. It had a giant head with enormous eyes and the longest, curliest eyelashes. But you didn't look through them because the head was so ginormous – there was a peephole in the neck to see out of. Attached to the head was a large piece of fabric for the body. The costume also had two pairs of fluffy, white and brown trousers with elastic braces to hold them up. We couldn't wait to get them on. I was starting to think that maybe this was going to be way more fun than being a narrator. Narrators only ever get to wear a smart shirt and tie.

'Who's going to be in the front then?' asked Miss Loretta, holding up the giant cow-head.

'Me! Me!' Jimmy was bouncing all over the place.

'I think I should be. I *am* the oldest,' I said. Only by seventeen minutes and forty-two seconds, but it still counts.

Jimmy stopped bouncing and scowled at me. His face turned to thunder. Miss Loretta began to get twitchy. We both knew what that meant. Jimmy was about to throw a wobbly.

'Shall we let Jimmy give it a try?' she asked me.

'Not as if I have much choice, is it?'

'Well, you are such a sensible girl, Cally. I tell you what, I'll give you a table-point for being considerate.'

Typical. Jimmy always gets his own way.

'Right, now then,' said Miss Loretta, lifting up the head and trying to make some sense of it. 'So, Jimmy, you stand up straight and Cally, you bend down and put your hands round Jimmy's waist.'

'Urrrgh. No way! She's not cuddling me,' protested Jimmy.

'As if I'd want to anyway.'

Miss Loretta rolled her eyes. 'How about, Cally, you just hold on to his belt.'

So, we did that, and then Miss Loretta lifted the cow-head onto Jimmy and pulled the fabric body over the two of us.

'It stinks in here,' said Jimmy. 'Sort of like dirty old washing.'

'You'd know all about that then, wouldn't

you? It's not as if it isn't thrown about all over your flea-pit of a bedroom.'

'Right then, that's enough, you two,' interrupted Miss Loretta, her voice becoming more high-pitched. 'Let's try walking forward. Left, right, left . . . oh dear!'

We hadn't even managed a single step and we were already crashing to the ground.

'Look what you're doing, you spoon!' I yelled. This was going to be impossible.

'It was your fault. You pulled me to the floor!' muffled the cow-head.

'You're the one doing the pulling. You're the one who's at the front!'

'Come along now,' said Miss Loretta, helping us back to our feet. 'Let's try again. We'll take it really slowly to start with.'

Jimmy doesn't do 'slowly'. He is bouncier than Tigger times two-hundred. But somehow Miss Loretta managed to pull us back together.

'OK, then. Let's start again. Just stand

 98

really still on the spot and lift your left leg up in the air.'

We did as Miss Loretta said.

'Now put it down in front of you, ever so carefully.'

We did that too.

'Now lift your right leg.'

Yep.

'Now put that one down as well.'

We did it. We'd done a step. Together. And in time!

Miss Loretta carried on talking us through our steps, very gradually building it up, so that, with a lot of practice and a few more bumps and stumbles, we were at last managing to walk all the way to the end of the corridor and back.

Sometimes, people would pass by and I could hear them shriek or laugh. I wished I could see the looks on their faces, but being the back-end of a pantomime cow, you don't exactly get to see that much – just the ground, two pairs of feet or Jimmy's bottom. I concentrated on looking down.

Just as things were finally going well, Jimmy went and did the worst thing ever.

'Jimmmmmyyyyyyyyyy! That's disgusting!' I wailed, collapsing to the ground and frantically scrabbling out of the cow costume, gasping for air. He'd only gone and . . . you know . . . let one go.

'I think we'll call it a day,' sighed Miss Loretta. It was nearly playtime anyway, and she definitely looked very ready for her tea break.

Getting Michelle to dance was the real challenge. We practised every day after school in the kitchen when we got home. Yiayia sewed two old sheets together and cut eye-holes in them so that the rehearsals could be more realistic. It was Yiayia's idea too that we should do Greek dancing. The steps are simpler than the hip-hop moves Jimmy had come up with. 'Step together – bend your knees – step to the side – kick your leg – step together – bend your knees . . .' Yiayia called out the instructions, clicking her fingers to the beat as we did our best to keep in time to the tune from *Zorba the Greek*. By the end of the week, we'd really got the hang of it and Yiayia was dancing alongside us, arms stretched out and whooping,

We practised the show a lot at school and then came the afternoon of the final dress rehearsal. All the narrators were lined up along the front of the stage; the main characters were waiting behind the curtains at the sides; Miss Loretta was sitting at the front with a script, ready to prompt anyone if they got stuck; Mitch Moran, who was in charge of the music, was on standby at the sound system, looking cool with his headphones on; Mrs Wright was at the back of the hall to make sure everyone was speaking loudly; we'd all learned the songs; all the props were in place. It was going to be great.

And actually it was. Until . . .

'Jimmy! Jimmy! Slow down, you're going too fast,' I panicked. 'We're gonna fallll!'

It was in the middle of *Zorba the Greek*, when the music gets to the speedy-up part.

Everything had been going really well and we'd rehearsed our part so many times at home, but not on the stage itself. I'm not sure exactly what went wrong because it all happened so quickly. Jimmy must have misjudged the space or something. All I know is that one minute we were going, step together – bend your knees – step to the side – kick your leg, and the next thing, Jimmy was flying off the stage and dragging me down with him. We landed in a heap on the floor. With a very big bump. And it hurt.

It really hurt. I couldn't even yell at Jimmy, I was in that much pain. It was my ankle. It felt like something was stabbing right through it. All I could do was cry.

I think Jimmy was OK because he scrambled out of Michelle and pulled the material off me, saying, 'Sorry, Sis. Sorry, Sis,' over and over again. Then all the other kids started crowding around and asking if we were still alive and everything. *Zorba the Greek* continued over the loudspeaker, getting faster and faster.

'Mitch! Will you *please* turn off that godforsaken music!' screeched Mrs Wright. I'd never heard her raise her voice like that before. 'Miss Loretta, take everyone outside for some extra play. Thank you. Nina Wilinska, go to the office and send for Mrs Johnston. Please.' Mrs Johnston does first aid and lost property.

Yiayia had to come and take us home early because of my ankle. Jimmy had grazed his hands a bit, but apart from that, he was OK. But me. I was in proper pain. We had to get a taxi because I was limping so badly.

'You'll be all right for tomorrow though, won't you?' asked Jimmy, who was being the quietest I'd ever known him to be. I wasn't sure if it was me he was more worried about, or Michelle. How was he going to get to show off in a dancing cow in assembly without his other half?

I hoped I'd be all right too. Mum had asked for the whole morning off work so she could be there, and Dad was coming as well. They can still do things like that together, for our sake. They get along OK most of the time. Even when they split up, there hadn't been any huge rows like Lauren Bennett's parents have. Dad just said he'd got tired. I'm not sure what being tired has got to do with it. Mum just said they had grown apart. Whatever that means. Yiayia said it was because Mum should have married a nice Greek boy.

But I wasn't all right. I kept waking up through the night from the throbbing in my ankle, and Mum had to give me two lots of Calpol. And the next morning, the morning of

107

the big day, my ankle was double its normal size and black, blue, purple and yellow all at once. And OMG did it hurt.

Everyone gathered around my bed, staring at my monstrous leg.

'I can't even step on it,' I winced.

'Lucky I've got the morning off, isn't it?' said Mum, running her hand through my hair. 'Come on, let's help you get dressed and we'll get you to A&E. This definitely needs an X-ray.'

'But . . . but . . . what about the assembly?' stammered Jimmy.

'It's all right. Yiayia can go ahead with you to school. Hopefully they won't keep us waiting at the hospital for ever. We might still be able to catch up with you in time to see the play. It doesn't start until ten thirty,' said Mum.

'But . . . but . . . what about Michelle?' said Jimmy.

'Yiayia will just have to explain. Mrs Wright

will understand. She saw what happened to Cally yesterday. Maybe they can get someone else to take Cally's place,' said Mum.

'How's anyone ever going to be able to do that? It took me and Cally all week to learn those moves. Who's going to be able to do *Zorba the Greek* in five minutes flat? And nobody wants to dance with me anyway.'

For once, Jimmy was absolutely right. There's no way anyone could step in and take my part. Jimmy's lip was beginning to wobble.

Oh dear, now was not the time for one of his meltdowns. Yiayia hurried him out of the room to get him ready for school. Mum helped me into my clothes. Then, leaning on her shoulder and hopping on one leg, I made it to the landing. I had to shuffle down the stairs on my bottom though. I tried really hard not to bump my bad leg on anything, because every time I did, the pain would shoot all the way up to my eyeballs.

On the way to the hospital, Mum told me to phone Dad to let him know what was going on.

'Shall I put him on speaker, Mum?'

'No, it's OK. You talk to him. There's a good girl.'

Dad picked up the phone pretty quick. He thought it was Mum at first, because I was ringing from her phone. I haven't got a phone yet. I've been asking for one for ages. Dad says he'll get me and Jimmy one, but Mum won't let

 110

him. She says we're too young and Jimmy has far too much screen-time as it is.

'Hi, Dad . . . No, it's me, Mum's driving . . . No, no, the play *is* today, the thing is, I've had a bit of an accident . . . No, it's all right really, just my leg . . . Yes, Mum's taking me to the hospital to have it checked out . . . What? . . . Wait a minute . . .' I turned to talk to Mum, 'Dad says do we want him to come to the hospital as well?'

'No, no,' said Mum, waving the phone away, 'tell him everything's under control and to go to the school as planned, so he can be there for Jimmy.'

I turned back to talk to Dad down the phone, 'Mum says everything's under control, and you need to go to the school to watch Jimmy . . . Yes, we're sure . . . Yes . . . I'll be OK . . . it's not so bad . . .' I was lying, of course, but I didn't want to worry Dad. 'Yes . . . thanks, Dad . . . Hopefully . . . yes . . . I love you, too, lots . . . Yes, like Jelly Tots,' and then the call ended.

When we got to the hospital, Mum scanned the rows of plastic blue chairs in the waiting area. 'Not too busy here, at least,' she said. One of the porters spotted me leaning on my mum and he came over with a wheelchair. Then Mum went up to the receptionist and checked us in.

'It shouldn't be too long,' the receptionist said. 'There's a children's area you can wait in, if you like?' she said, nodding to a space around the corner which had a broken plastic green fence around it and a few even more broken toys inside, and a table with a twisted bead-rack. It didn't exactly look inviting for a toddler, never mind me. I mean, I *am* in Year Five.

'I think we'll just wait here, thank you,' said Mum and she wheeled me over to the end of the front row of blue chairs. 'There's a little café over there. How about I get you a hot chocolate? They might even have doughnuts, if you'd like one?'

That definitely cheered me up. Mum never

gets us doughnuts. Even when Jimmy does his begging act. She says they're far too sugary and unhealthy. The worst thing for Jimmy's condition. But Jimmy wasn't there. And Mum was getting me one, to have with my hot chocolate. And I realised that this was possibly the first time in forever that I had had my mum all to myself. OK, it probably would have been better not to have to go through the agony of a busted ankle to get her attention, but it did feel good. Just to be me and her. Just for a bit.

Luckily we didn't wait too long for an X-ray, which Mum said was a miracle. It turned out that my ankle wasn't broken either. Just very badly sprained. The doctor thought there might be a sign of the tiniest sliver of a fracture, so we would have to come back for another scan in two weeks. Until then, they put one of those giant boot thingies with the Velcro straps on me and gave me a pair of crutches. They said to take paracetamol for the pain and to keep the pressure off the foot. And that was it. We were free to go.

Mum checked her watch, 'Ten past ten. If we get a wriggle on, we might just make it.'

Mastering the crutches at lightning speed, we made a hop, skip and a jump to Mum's car and sped off for school. I wondered how Jimmy and Michelle were getting on. I hoped they'd managed to find a decent sub. If anyone could sort it, Mrs It'll-be-all-Wright-on-the-Night would. But I doubted it – and I felt really sad for Jimmy.

 114

We arrived just in time. Mrs Johnston was on the door showing in the last of the parents. Her eyes popped out of her head when she saw me hopping in on my crutches.

'My goodness, Cally. You really did take a nasty tumble, didn't you? Now then, the hall's rather crowded, but let's see if we can find you a special chair at the side.'

The hall was jam-packed with parents. We were looking about for Yiayia, but we couldn't see her for all the people.

'You know your Yiayia. She's probably managed to wangle herself a seat right at the front. She was here really early after all. Don't worry, we'll find her afterwards,' said Mum.

I spotted Dad though. He was standing at the back. He's very tall and doesn't like to be in anyone's way. 'Dad! Dad!' I shouted across the audience. But he couldn't hear me. Mum said, 'Shhhh. It's about to start.'

I was dying for Michelle to come on. Who

 115

had they got to replace me? Would whoever it was be able to step in time with Jimmy? Would they be able to make the cow dance at such short notice?

My best friend Aisha stood up in her smart shirt and tie and began narrating the bit where Michelle would make her entrance:

> Jack was a young lad who lived in a village with his mother. They were very poor. So poor in fact, that it came to be that Jack must sell the last thing of value that they owned. Their beloved cow, Michelle ...

And on strode Michelle. Everyone in the audience laughed. Some even started clapping. I was just seriously willing Jimmy, and whoever his new partner was, to be OK. But actually, they appeared to be doing unbelievably well. They were a little bit wobbly at first, but not bad at all for beginners. Who was it with Jimmy

under that fluffy, white and brown body? Well done them, anyway.

But I knew the real test was yet to come. Michelle had to dance for the giant. That big moment had been saved for the grand finale.

And so, Michelle nervously stood before the giant, who sat moodily on his colossal throne, waiting to be entertained . . .

Michelle wasn't the only nervous one. I was biting my nails to bits. Please let them be OK. Please let them be OK.

Mitch Moran cued the music. There was a ripple of amusement through the audience as some of the parents recognised the opening notes to *Zorba the Greek*. And Michelle began to dance.

Step together – bend your knees – step to the side – kick your leg – step together – bend your knees . . .

 118

She was doing it. Michelle was actually dancing. And she was dancing amazingly. Everyone was cheering and laughing and clapping along. Really, who was that in there with Jimmy? They were so good. The music kept going, getting faster and faster, and still Michelle stepped in time and kept to the beat.

And when it came to the end, everyone in the audience got to their feet and gave Michelle a massive round of applause.

And that was when my Yiayia climbed out of the back of the dancing cow, slapped her thigh and whooped,

Jimmy clambered out from underneath Michelle's head too. He took Yiayia's hand, led her to the front of the stage and Mrs Wright said, 'Ladies and gentlemen, giants and juniors, let's hear it for Year Five and our special guest star, the one and only, Yiayia!' And the audience went wild as Jimmy and Yiayia took their bow.

That assembly would go down in history. And all because of my Yiayia. My sweet, kind, slightly crazy, Yiayia.

'Right then, kids,' said Mum as we gathered around the table for Sunday lunch, 'we need to sort out what we're doing for your tenth birthday this year.'

Yiayia almost spat out her soup, 'How they get to be ten already?'

'I know!' whistled Mum. 'Double digits, eh? We'll have to make it special.'

'I want a football party,' demanded Jimmy, leaping out of his seat.

Of course he did. He's obsessed with football. Ever since he found out we were born at Queen

 127

Charlotte's Hospital, which is right by the QPR stadium, he's been QPR mad. It's not one of the flashier teams like Man U or Liverpool, but they're a team that Dad doesn't mind taking us along to sometimes when we go to stay with him at the weekends. Chelsea is closer to Clapham, but Dad says that the Premier League teams are all about the money.

I don't mind football that much, but I didn't want yet another birthday party that involved loads of running about. We always have those, because Jimmy is such an 'active' boy. That's the polite word grown-ups use for when he's being 'hyper'. For our ninth birthday, we had a Lazer Tag party, for our eighth, we had a trampoline party, our seventh had been a disco, on our sixth birthday, we went to the One O'Clock Club because there was an enormous pirate ship in it and Jimmy was crazy about pirates that year. Our younger birthdays involved hiring out some sort of hall where everyone

 128

ran around for two hours, bursting balloons and play-fighting. I'd have liked to have done more party games, but I remember Mum giving up after Musical Bumps, because that was the only one that Jimmy liked. Musical Statues was totally out of the question with Jimmy because he can't stand still and Musical Chairs was far too dangerous to even think about – Musical Accident-Waiting-to-Happen, Mum called it.

'I don't want a football party,' I said.

'Football! Football! Football!' Jimmy chanted.

'Well, what would you like instead?' asked Mum.

'I want to have all my friends round, like Candice Solomon did for hers. I want us to do makeovers and each other's hair and stuff like that for a change . . .'

Yiayia choked on her soup for real then. 'But Jimmy is boy. He not want that, is he?'

Jimmy was too busy singing, 'I'm Rangers till I die, I'm Rangers till I die, I know I am, I'm sure I am, I'm Rangers till I die.'

'If you don't shut it, Jimmy, I might just kill you myself,' I snapped.

'Now, now, Calista . . .' sighed Mum.

'But it's not fair. Why is it always about Jimmy? Why does he always get what *he* wants? Why do I even have to share my birthday with him anyway? For once in my life, why can't I have my own birthday all to myself?'

'Because you is twins, isn't it?' said Yiayia.

'We love you Rangers, we do, we love you

130

Rangers, we do . . .' Jimmy was still singing at the top of his voice.

Mum put her head in her hands and sighed. This wasn't getting us anywhere. Until . . . until . . . Mum suddenly looked up, her eyes shining. 'I've got it!' she said. 'How about we do a birthday split. Jimmy can have his football party outside in the garden . . .'

'Goooooooaaaaaaaaaaalllllllll!' cheered Jimmy.

'. . . and Cally can have her makeover fashion party upstairs. How about that, then?' suggested Mum.

I looked at Jimmy. Jimmy looked at me.

'But . . . but . . .' said Jimmy, not singing now. 'But we always have our birthdays together.'

'Well, this time we're not,' I said, sticking my nose in the air. And that was that. It was decided. Two separate birthdays, it would be.

Sorting out a double birthday turned out to be trickier than we had realised. Me and Jimmy are in the same class, so we share a lot of our friends. Who would go to which party? Yiayia thought it was obvious. The boys would go to Jimmy's one and the girls would come to mine. But we don't live in the dinosaur age anymore and there were plenty of girls who'd want to play football just as much as the boys. My best friend Aisha would for starters. She isn't into painting her nails or wearing sparkly unicorn tops. Was I supposed to make her choose?

'I think we'll have to,' said Mum. 'We'll put on the invitations that there's a choice between football or fashion and the reply slip can include a box to tick. I'm sure it will work out just fine.'

 132

So that's what we did. We designed the invitations in two halves, split down the middle. Goals and grit on one side and glamour and glitter on the other. We couldn't wait to give them out at school the next day. Mum said we could invite everyone in the class. She always makes a big effort for our birthday because she says it's double special. She puts decorations everywhere with bunting and streamers and loads of balloons. Mum makes the most amazing cakes too – she could be on one of those TV bake-off shows. And this year we were getting one each. Jimmy's was going to be a football pitch and mine was going to be a fashion-show catwalk.

When the replies came back, Yiayia was pretty much proved right after all, because every single boy had ticked 'Football' and all the girls, except for Aisha, wanted to come to my makeover party. So that was settled.

The night before our birthday we went to

stay at Dad's. I would have liked him to have come to our party, but he said, 'Best not,' which was a bit sad. So, the plan was to go out for burgers after school on the Friday and then have a sleepover at his flat – that way we'd wake up and have our actual birthday morning with him. Which was still kind of special. If you think about it, it can almost be a bonus when your parents split up. Double birthday treats. Double holidays. Double presents. Maybe. But I do miss Dad when he's not there.

Dad took us to Gastro Grill, by Clapham Common – it's one of those posh burger places that do the biggest, juiciest half-pounders, and extra creamy milkshakes that come in giant silver flasks with curly-whirly straws. It's even got its own ice-cream station with a pump that you can use yourself to squeeze out as much ice cream as you like, and there's a cart with a million different types of sprinkles to choose from. Jimmy's not meant to have that much

 134

sugar, but I knew Dad would let him off because it was nearly our birthday. Mum says Dad's a soft touch and he shouldn't spoil us so much. But we weren't complaining.

The waitress had Jimmy all worked out before we'd hardly got through the door. There was a sign on a stand that said, 'Please wait to be seated' and Jimmy was doing that thing of hopping from one foot to the other that he does whenever he's extra excited.

The waitress led us to a booth furthest away from anyone else at the back of the restaurant. She went to hand us each a menu. She was about to give me and Jimmy the kids' one and a pot of crayons, but the look of horror on our faces made Dad rush to tell the waitress, 'It's their tenth birthday. They eat like horses these days. We'll all have the grown-ups' menus please.'

The waitress made a point of noticing Jimmy drumming on the table with his knife and fork. I could tell she was thinking, *he might*

eat like a grown-up but it's a shame he doesn't act like one. Jimmy's table manners are still what Mum calls a 'work-in-progress'. We don't go to restaurants much because of them.

The waitress gave us the proper menus and said, 'Can I get you any drinks while you're deciding?'

'Just tap water all round, please, I think,' said Dad.

'Oh! But what about the milkshakes?' protested Jimmy.

'If you want to go to the ice-cream station afterwards, I think that will be enough, Jimmy,' said Dad.

Dad was right of course. I really wanted a milkshake too. But if Jimmy couldn't have one, then I couldn't either. Wouldn't be fair on him otherwise. I always have to suffer because of Jimmy. Not exactly fair on me either, is it?

'Maybe we'll stop using the table as a drum kit, Jimmy. You're a big boy now,' said Dad.

Jimmy put down his knife and fork and started unscrewing the lids off the salt and pepper pots instead.

The waitress returned and plonked down three glasses in the middle of the table and a jug of water. It had a load of mint leaves in it and a slice of lime. Posh burger place. See.

'Urgh, the water's got some kind of jungle growing out of it,' said Jimmy, trying to be funny. Not.

He reached over to grab a glass, but

practically climbed up on the table to do so and ended up skidding off the bench and diving forwards, sending the whole jug of jungle water flying, along with the salt and pepper pots too, which still had their lids off, so they got emptied into the whole mess as well.

If the waitress had been from a cartoon, steam would have come out of her ears at that moment.

'I'm so dreadfully sorry,' said Dad. 'Please. If you have a mop and bucket. Some cloths. We'll clean it up of course.'

'Not to worry,' the waitress said through gritted teeth. 'If you'd like to move over to the next booth, we'll get it sorted.'

I gave Jimmy the biggest glare and dragged him by the elbow to where the waitress wanted us to go. Why did he always have to make us all look so bad?

'It was an accident,' muttered Jimmy. Those world-famous words of his. His face was red though and he buried himself into his menu once we'd sat down again, so I could tell even he felt ashamed.

The waitress returned with a notepad and pen, and one of those smiles where someone's mouth is smiling but the rest of their face isn't. 'Can I take your order?' she said.

'I'll have the Classic Beef, medium rare, with regular fries, please,' said Dad.

'And please can I have the Classic Chicken, with regular fries too,' I said.

Jimmy was still studying the menu, his tongue sticking out the side of his mouth as he concentrated, as usual. 'Ha ha! They've got one called The Taxi Driver.'

They had one called The Jumpin' Jack as well. I was surprised he hadn't automatically gone for that one. 'Just hurry up and choose, Jimmy,' I said.

The look on the waitress's face was saying something like that too.

'OK . . . so . . . please can I have . . . I'll have the Mighty Cheese, but without the cheese . . . no wait . . . no . . . yes . . . without the cheese . . .'

141

'How can it be a Mighty Cheese without the cheese? That's the whole point of it, you dumbo!' I said, rolling my eyes.

'Don't call him that, Cals,' said Dad.

'OK . . . so . . . the Mighty Cheese without the cheese . . .' continued Jimmy, 'and no lettuce or onions . . . and . . . wait . . . yeah . . . no relish or tomato either . . .'

The waitress pressed her pen really hard into her notepad and said, 'So that will be a plain burger then for the young man?'

'Yes. I think that would be right. Thank you,' said Dad. 'And regular fries for him too, please.'

The burgers arrived and they were great. We were starving by then and wiped them out really quick. Even Jimmy managed to get through his with minimum disaster – just a bit of a squirty tomato sauce explosion halfway through, but not too bad, for him.

And then the time had come! The ice-cream station.

'I'm first,' I insisted. 'I'm the oldest.' I know, only by seventeen minutes and forty-two seconds, but it still counts.

Jimmy sighed and let me go ahead, whilst he did his hopping from one foot to the next thing again. As I was squirting ice cream out of the pump into my bowl, I could see him sneaking the jelly beans out of the sprinkles cart. 'Don't let the waitress see you picking at them. You're supposed to use the scoop.'

When I'd finished, I moved over to get my sprinkles and Jimmy took his turn. He yanked the pump down and cheered as the ice cream came twisting out.

'OK, that's enough, Jimmy. Switch it off now.'

Jimmy tried to push the pump back up, but it kept falling down.

'I can't!' he panicked.

'What do you mean? Quick, get another bowl, that one's overflowing.'

 143

The ice-cream was going everywhere.

'The handle's got all loose. It keeps falling down,' said Jimmy.

'What? You've broken the ice-cream station, as well? The waitress is going to kill you.'

I went over and pushed the handle back up. But it wouldn't stay there when I let go.

'What are we going to do?' said Jimmy.

'You mean, what are *you* going to do? You're the one who busted it.'

'It was an accident!'

How many times.

'Wait . . . I've got an idea . . .' said Jimmy, rummaging around in his pockets and pulling out a lump of Blu Tack. He's always picking it off from the back of Mrs Wright's displays in the classroom. 'It might just work . . .'

Jimmy squished the Blu Tack around the pump handle. It seemed to hold it in place. But for how long?

'Quick, let's get out of here,' said Jimmy.

We rushed back to our table.

'Dad, shall we go now?' I said.

'But you haven't had your ice cream yet.'

'It's not that nice,' I said.

'Yeah. It's all sort of thin,' added Jimmy.

'Yeah. You know, runny.'

'Yeah, runny and thin. And a bit flat tasting.'

Flat tasting? Jimmy always has to take things too far.

'Let's just get the bill,' I said.

Dad looked puzzled. 'If you're sure?'

I could see the handle of the ice-cream station out of the corner of my eye. Please let it hold up. Please let it hold up.

The waitress brought us the bill double quick. Pretty keen to finish with our table too no doubt. Dad paid and we grabbed our coats and made a dash for it.

'What's the hurry?' said Dad, chasing after us.

We rushed out of the door, and just as we

 146

reached the safety of outside, we heard a shriek coming from the restaurant. Through the window we could see a river of ice cream overflowing from the pump. And one fuming waitress.

Dad looked at us with a frown. I smiled sweetly back up at him. Jimmy shrugged his shoulders.

'Come on, then. Let's get you back to the flat,' Dad said.

When we got to Dad's, he said we could stay up for a bit, but not too late as we didn't want to be tired for our birthday party the next day. So we played a quick game of Monopoly before getting into our pyjamas. I know Monopoly's not really a short game for anyone normal, but if you're playing with Jimmy it never lasts that long. Monopoly with Jimmy is basically a row over who's going to be the car, and him ending up getting his own way with me always having to be the ship, followed by a few rounds of him cheating by trying to get away with not landing on any of our properties and nicking extra £100s from the bank whenever he passes go, and then it all ends with him going off in a sulk whenever someone else gets to buy Mayfair. So that's basically what happened until it was time to brush our teeth and get into our bunkbeds.

Dad came to say goodnight. 'Now that

 148

you're very nearly almost ten, does that mean we're too old for a snuzzle?'

'Never,' I said, reaching out my arms. Dad gave me the biggest, squeeziest hug.

As Jimmy was on the top bunk, it wasn't so easy to get up there for a cuddle, so they did their special complicated goodnight high-five thing instead.

'Night, night, my twinvincibles,' said Dad.

'Night, night, Dad.'

But it took us ages to get to sleep. We were way too excited. Tomorrow was our actual birthday and it was going to be brilliant.

We must have eventually drifted off though because the next thing I knew it was morning, and we were ten!

When I say morning, I mean literally the crack of dawn, cos Jimmy woke up extra super early that day. My twin Jimmy hollering, 'Woooooooooooooooo hooooooooooooooooo!!!!!' was what I woke up to on my tenth birthday, along

 149

with him dive-bombing off the top bunk and dragging me out of bed to go and get Dad.

We woke Dad up really early, but for once he didn't mind and he looked nearly as excited about our presents as we were. He must have stayed up the night before to wrap them because one of them was really massive and took up half the lounge. It was for Jimmy of course. He *would* get the biggest present.

'Go on, then,' smiled Dad.

Not that Jimmy needed any encouragement. He was already scrambling all over the giant present, ripping off the paper and saying, 'What is it? What is it?'

It was a pair of goal posts.

'Whoahhhhhhhh that's so siiiiiiiiick!'

'For your party,' said Dad. 'I can set them up for you in your garden.'

Meanwhile, I'd opened mine. It was a chemistry set so I could experiment with potions – real ones with crystals and science ingredients.

'There's one more each,' said Dad, reaching for another two presents. Jimmy opened his first again. 'Yesssssssss! A QPR top. And it's got my name on the back of it and everything. Thanks, Dad.'

'It's an official one from the club shop. Thought you might like to wear it for your party,' Dad said.

'Totally!' said Jimmy.

'And last, but not least,' said Dad, handing me my other gift that looked like it might be a box of make-up maybe, or a jewellery box perhaps, for my party too? 'Now they say, the best things come in small packages. A grown-up present for my grown-up girl,' he said.

I unwrapped the paper. I couldn't believe it.

'OMG!'

'OMG!!!!! You're the best dad, ever!' It was a smartphone.

'Well, that way you can call me whenever you need to. And you'll be needing it as you get more independent, I thought,' said Dad.

'That's not fair. What about meeeeeeeeee?' said Jimmy.

'Stop complaining. You got the biggest present, didn't you?' I reminded him.

'It's for both of you, really,' explained Dad. 'It's just, well, let's say, Cally's in charge of it. You're together most of the time anyway. It would be a bit silly to get two now, wouldn't it? And you've got your tablet at home as well, haven't you, Jimmy?'

Jimmy shrugged, 'I suppose.'

After a special birthday breakfast (Dad makes the best pancakes), we headed back home to get ready for our party. Me and Jimmy couldn't wait to see Mum and Yiayia and show them our presents, and to see all the decorations and the party food and everything.

Mum and Yiayia were there at the front door to welcome us. Dad stood on the doorstep holding on to Jimmy's goalposts. 'Hi. Thought I might step out into the garden and set these up,' he offered.

'Oh no, it's OK. I've got help . . .' said Mum.

And that was when Grant appeared in the hallway too, looking all heroic. Who invited *him* to our birthday?

'Grant's very kindly brought over some extra tables and chairs,' said Mum.

'All right, mate?' said Grant.

Dad just nodded.

Yiayia folded her arms and shuffled off to the kitchen.

 154

Dad looked up and down the hall. He was noticing the new DIY Express wallpaper that Grant had put up too, I could tell.

'Well . . . er . . . yes . . . OK. I'll be off now then . . .' he said, giving me and Jimmy one last kiss and a quick hug. 'Have a great day, kids.'

I watched Dad walk back to his car. I waved goodbye, but I don't think he saw because he was looking more at the ground by then. Closing the front door, I turned round to Mum and said, 'Dad got me this phone. See?'

I thought she might get a bit mad, but Mum just shook her head and muttered something about Dad having been too extravagant and how much easier it was to buy a couple of expensive gifts than it was to organise an entire party.

But we were all too busy with the excitement of the big birthday extravaganza to think about stuff like that for long. Jimmy was that bouncy, Mum ended up having to shut him outside in the garden so she could get the rest of the preparations done. He didn't seem to mind though – Grant was fixing up the goalposts and Jimmy was more than happy to have a kickabout with his imaginary friends until our actual ones arrived.

I took over from Yiayia blowing up the

balloons because it looked as if she was running out of puff. 'You are good girl, Calista mou. When we finish balloon we put up flags, yes?'

'What flags do you mean, Yiayia? Mum's already done the bunting,' I said.

'This flags,' she said, proudly whipping out a string of Cyprus flags from her shopping trolley as if she were some sort of Greek magician. There were some with the Greece flag too, blue and white stripes. 'Same like QPR colour, you see?' said Yiayia. 'I get from St Andrew's Day festival at church.'

Yiayia was too cute sometimes. She looked so pleased with herself, I just said, 'OK then. We'll put them up. Sure.'

Yiayia's specialities didn't stop there either. She'd insisted on making a batch of meatballs and a tray-load of baklava for the party too. Cocktail sausages and cupcakes were more everyone's thing, but hopefully my friends would like Yiayia's Greek food as well.

 157

At last it was time for the guests to arrive. Yiayia was in charge of answering the door. She stood there under the balloons, checking everyone's invitations, like a pocket-sized bodyguard in a shiny pink party hat with a yellow feather sticking out of it. She had one of those party-horn-blower things between her teeth, and every time someone arrived, she gave it a blast and said, 'Football or Fashion?' then she'd direct our friends either out into the garden or up to my room.

It was great fun upstairs. We painted our nails, did glitter tattoos, sprayed coloured streaks into our hair and pinned it up with sparkly clips and JoJo bows. Candice did really cool plaits for some of the girls too. We were even allowed make-up. Aisha had bought me a massive carousel set with a million different coloured eye shadows and lip glosses – I easily forgave her for choosing Jimmy's party over mine after that. It was the best present.

We played music and danced around under the unicorn disco light ball that Yiayia had given me.

I was having a good time. I really was. And for once I was getting exactly what I wanted for my birthday. My very own party all to myself.

It was what I wanted, wasn't it? Why was it then, why was it that something wasn't quite 100 per cent about it? Why didn't it quite feel right? It was as if there was something missing? I don't know why. We had everything. Music. Make-up. Accessories. Friends. Ace presents. So what was it that was missing?

THUD! A football slammed against the window, leaving a muddy mark against the pane.

Jimmy.

I ran over to the window and looked down onto the garden. There was Jimmy, standing in the middle of the football pitch, staring up at the window. He was surrounded by Aisha and all the boys from our class, but somehow he looked alone. Everyone was running around him, but for once Jimmy was the one standing still. He just stood there. Looking up at my bedroom window.

I gave him a little wave.

He gave me a little wave back.

 160

'Cally! What you doing over there? Come back and show us how to work this Karaoke machine . . .' My friends were calling me. And so I slipped away from the window and went back to my own separate party.

But not long after that, Jimmy's face appeared round my bedroom door.

'Jimmmmmyyyyy!' cried Nina, 'What are you doing here?'

'Just wanted to see what it was like up here,' he shrugged, stepping into the room.

'If you're so interested in our makeover party, how about we really show you?' I said, waving a Very Berry lip gloss wand.

And before he knew what was happening, we'd surrounded Jimmy, mischief written all over our faces.

'Wh . . . wh . . . what you doing?' stammered Jimmy.

'We're getting you ready for the catwalk,' I grinned, whipping off his QPR shirt and

 162

replacing it with a rainbow sparkly dress.

Everyone shrieked with laughter.

Jimmy looked a bit confused, but I think he saw the funny side too because he kind of gave in and let us get on with it.

We shoved a pair of glittery deely boppers on his head and a pink feather boa around his neck.

'Aww, he looks amazing!'

'It suits you, Jimmy!'

And then we got busy with hair and make-up. Glossy lipstick, blue eye shadow, green mascara and a unicorn glitter-tattoo on his cheek to complete the look.

'He looks really pretty!'

'He actually looks like you now, Cally.'

'Hey, Cally, why don't we dress you up as Jimmy?'

'Grab his QPR kit.'

And before we knew it, I was looking like Jimmy and Jimmy was looking like me.

 163

Jimmy started strutting round the room like a supermodel, one hand on his hip, the other swishing by his side. Every now and then, he'd stop, strike a pose and wiggle his bottom.

'You're a natural, Jimmy.'

'Hey, let's take this fashion show downstairs!'

'Yeah, let's do a party mash-up!'

The girls dashed downstairs to set it all up. They got everyone who was out in the garden to sit in rows either side of the lawn, making an aisle for the models to parade up and down. They put the music speaker on standby, ready for Jimmy's and my appearance. Whilst they did all this, me and Jimmy hid behind the curtains by the patio doors, waiting for our cue. It was just the two of us for the first time that day. Me and Jimmy, ready to face the rest of the world. Maybe that's why Jimmy got all serious for a second and said to me, 'You know, I'm glad we're doing our party as a mash-up. It didn't quite feel like it was properly my birthday out there in the garden without you.'

'Same.' I said. 'Same for me upstairs.'

'Anyway,' grinned Jimmy, 'I look loads better as a girl than you do.'

'Ha ha. Very funny, Dimitrina,' I said, giving him a shove.

And then Candice was announcing our grand entrance: 'And now, new on the fashion scene, but already causing quite a stir, please give it up for the sensational Cally and Jimmy!'

And out we burst though the curtains and into the garden, strutting, shimmying and posing like something out of London Fashion

Week. Everyone cheered and whooped and roared with laughter. All except for Yiayia, who practically fell off her chair in shock. She didn't know what to say. She just kept repeating, 'But Jimmy is boy, but Jimmy is boy,' over and over again.

But Jimmy was just Jimmy. Always up for a laugh. Always the centre of attention. The rest of us understood. Not least of all

Mum. Because when it came to singing *Happy Birthday*, and she brought out the cakes, she took one of the plastic QPR players from Jimmy's football pitch cake and placed it on my catwalk, and then she took a miniature unicorn from mine, and put it in goal on Jimmy's. The birthday mash-up was complete. Me and Jimmy were meant to celebrate our birthdays together. And as we blew out our ten candles, all at once, we held hands, closed our eyes and wished.

So now we are ten. Double digits. Jimmy will still be annoying. He will still always get most of the attention and be different in lots of ways. But we are still twins. And one thing we definitely agreed on for sure that day was – it had been the best birthday ever.